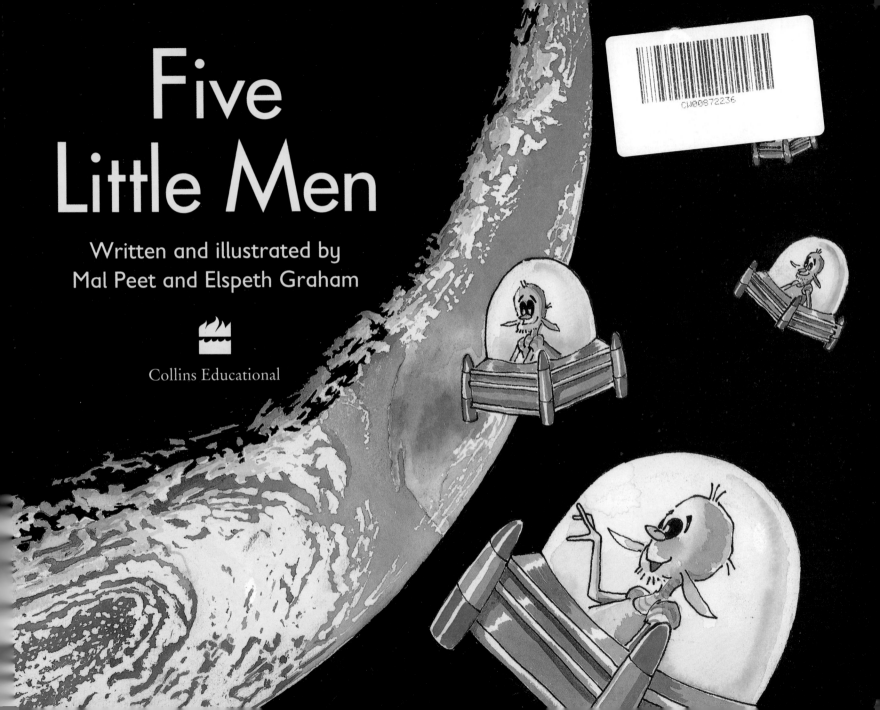

Five Little Men

Written and illustrated by
Mal Peet and Elspeth Graham

Collins Educational

Five little men in flying saucers
Flew round the Earth one day.
They looked left and right
And they didn't like the sight

So one man flew away.

whoosh

Four little men in flying saucers
Flew round the Earth one day.

They looked left and right
And they didn't like the sight

So one man flew away.

whoosh----

Three little men in flying saucers
Flew round the Earth one day.

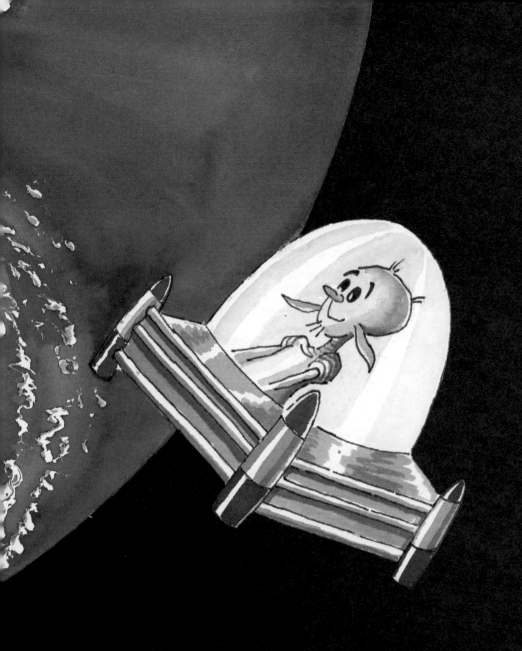

They looked left and right
And they didn't like the sight

10

So one man flew away.

whoosh.....

Two little men in flying saucers
Flew round the Earth one day.

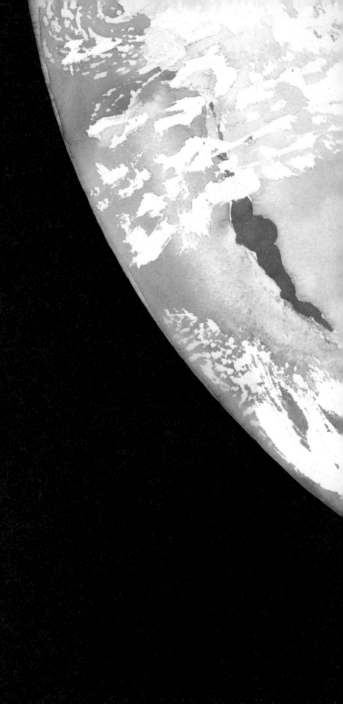

They looked left and right
And they didn't like the sight

One little man in a flying saucer
Flew round the Earth one day.

He looked left and right
And he didn't like the sight

So one man flew away.

whoosh...

Five little men in flying saucers
Flew back to their home far away.

Their friends gathered round
To see what they had found
Beyond the Milky Way.

They'd never seen such wonderful things!
They gasped and stared and gasped again

And said,
"Of all the worlds in all of space,
Earth must be the loveliest place!"

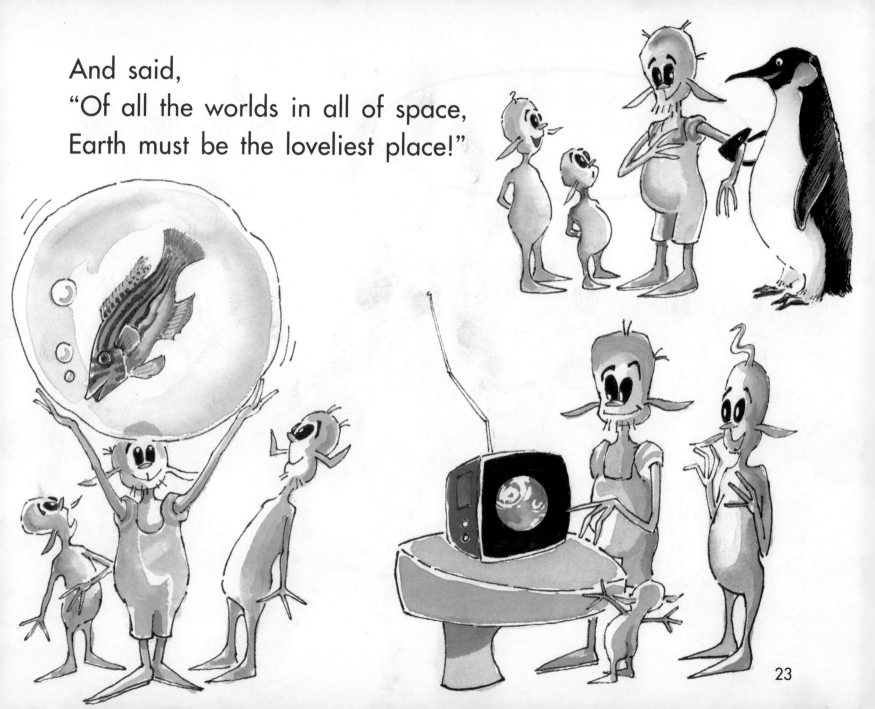